PUFFIN BOOKS

The Roundhill

Dick King-Smith served in the Grenadier Guards during the Second World War, and afterwards spent twenty years as a farmer in Gloucestershire, the county of his birth. Many of his stories are inspired by his farming experiences. Later he taught at a village primary school. His first book, *The Fox Busters*, was published in 1978. Since then he has written a great number of children's books, including *The Sheep-Pig* (winner of the *Guardian* Award and filmed as *Babe*), *Harry's Mad*, *Noah's Brother*, *The Hodgeheg*, *Martin's Mice*, *Ace*, *The Cuckoo Child* and *Harriet's Hare* (winner of the Children's Book Award in 1995). At the British Book Awards in 1992 he was voted Children's Author of the Year. He has three children, twelve grandchildren and two great-grandchildren, and lives now in a seventeenth-century cottage, only a short crow's-flight from the house where he was born.

D1366235

DICK KING-SMITH

THE ROUNDHILL

Illustrated by Sîan Bailey

PUFFIN BOOKS

PUFFIN BOOKS

Published by the Penguin Group
Penguin Books Ltd, 80 Strand, London WC2R 0RL, England
Penguin Putnam Inc., 375 Hudson Street, New York, New York 10014, USA
Penguin Books Australia Ltd, Ringwood, Victoria, Australia
Penguin Books Canada Ltd, 10 Alcorn Avenue, Toronto, Ontario, Canada M4V 3B2
Penguin Books India (P) Ltd, 11 Community Centre, Panchsheel Park, New Delhi – 110 017, India
Penguin Books (NZ) Ltd, Cnr Rosedale and Airborne Roads, Albany, Auckland, New Zealand
Penguin Books (South Africa) (Pty) Ltd, 24 Sturdee Avenue, Rosebank 2196 South Africa

Penguin Books Ltd, Registered Offices: 80 Strand, London WC2R 0RL, England

www.penguin.com

First published by Viking 2000
Published in Puffin Books 2001
3

Filmset in 14/17 Baskerville

Printed in England by Clays Ltd, St Ives plc

British Library Cataloguing in Publication Data
A CIP catalogue record for this book is available from the British Library

ISBN 0–141–30376–X

For Myrle

CHAPTER 1

The Roundhill itself was of no great size or height. A small dome topped with a little cluster of hardwood trees, it stood upon the ridge of one of the last southerly spurs of the Cotswolds. Silhouetted against the sky, it could easily be seen from a number of miles away.

To Evan, it was a magic place. The Grange, the

house in which he had been born in 1922, had a clear sight of it. When he was young someone had given him a compass for a present, and it seemed to Evan very important that the bearing of the Roundhill from his bedroom window was absolutely due east.

Now, in his teens, Evan sometimes said to himself that when he died – which won't be for an awfully long time, I hope, he thought – he wanted his grave to be in a part of the churchyard from which the little tree-capped hill would be clearly visible.

He judged that the Roundhill was two miles distant as the crow flew, though for him it meant a bike ride of nearer five miles to get there.

Evan's first action each morning, on getting out of bed, was to go to the window and look across at it.

Sometimes on dark winter mornings its shape would be hard to distinguish. Sometimes it would stand up dark before the glow of the sun rising behind it, sometimes it would show its customary green with a background of blue sky. Often it would seem to be a silver grey, sandwiched between low cloud above and mist rising from the river valley below. On a few days, in some years, snow painted the Roundhill white, save for its topknot of black trees. But always, even on mornings when thick fog or driving rain rendered it invisible, it was there, Evan knew, and he would gaze eastward towards its unseen shape as a pilgrim looks towards Mecca.

At fourteen, Evan did not think of himself as a religious person. His parents called themselves Christians, though (weddings and funerals apart) they only went to church on Christmas Day. Evan himself had been brought up by them to believe in God. It was something they seemed to expect of him, though they did little about it, leaving all that to school assemblies.

But believing in God, Evan found, wasn't all that easy. How on earth did people manage to believe in this – this what, person, thing, idea? – if they could not see him (Him, they said) or it or whatever.

Standing before the looking-glass in his

bedroom, Evan was in no doubt as to the identity of the figure who faced him: the figure of a tall thin pale boy with straight black hair, a lock of which fell across his forehead. That's me, he said to himself, I know me; and leaning on the bedroom window-sill in the morning, he could plainly see the ponies in the paddock below, the sheep and cattle in the fields beyond, the birds flying past, the trees, the hedges, that familiar shape on the skyline. Of all these he was sure, certain of their existence. But God?

And if there was one, supposedly a loving caring God, how come the news each day was so filled with cruelty and famine and war and disaster and death? How could you worship someone, something, which allowed, or perhaps was powerless to prevent, such horrors?

I'd like to think there was a God, I really would, he told himself. Perhaps one day I will.

In the meantime, I've got the Roundhill.

Evan's father, Charles Pennington, and his mother, Barbara, were a conventional English middle-class married couple. Charles was a lawyer by profession, and Barbara, as became a comfortably-off wife at that time – the summer of 1936 – looked after their house. Which is to say she employed servants to look after it, a cook and two housemaids and, outside, a gardener, leaving her free to amuse herself.

Frequent trips, in her own small car, to the nearest town, to do a little shopping and meet various women friends at a restaurant for mid-morning coffee, kept her occupied. There was also of course the responsibility of deciding what the cook should prepare for meals, of ensuring that the housemaids kept everything spotless and coped with the laundry and the ironing, and of arranging the flowers the gardener had grown.

Both parents, the busy father and the idle mother, were fond of their only child, again in a conventional way. Neither of them was demonstrative, considering displays of emotion – be they of joy or sorrow – to be best left to foreigners. So that a casual visitor to the

Pennington household would have seen no obvious signs of mutual affection, between man and wife, or between parent and child.

Evan, growing up in this atmosphere, had never actually thought of himself as unloved. He merely supposed that his parents' upper lips were generally too stiff to allow of such an action as a kiss, and was content, on occasions such as going away for a new term at boarding school, to receive a peck from his mother and a manly grasp of the hand from his father.

As a small boy, going back to school had made Evan unhappy. Each term it was a wrench to leave home. Below his bedroom window was a may tree where a song-thrush sang, and always, on the morning he was due to go, with his trunk and tuck-box ready packed, the thrush's song sounded so sweetly melancholy that Evan would feel a lump in his throat at the thought of leaving.

He would miss his parents of course, but that was only a small part of it. What he would really miss, what he would not see again for two or three months, was his home, and in particular his own room. It was a small bedroom, in the top storey of the tall old house, but it was very dear to him, especially because of that view from its window. As he grew older, he became much more matter-of-fact about returning to school, but always the very last thing he did before leaving was to stand by that window in his school uniform and look out, to pay a wordless farewell to the Roundhill.

By contrast, of course, the high point of the homeward journey at the end of each term was the moment when the car reached that particular spot from which he could first set eyes again on this, his favourite place. Once he could see it, all was right with the world.

CHAPTER 2

As well as looking at the Roundhill each day, Evan visited it, at least once, during school holidays.

To cycle to its foot, to climb its grassy slopes and stand upon its tree-topped crown, was something that he loved to do, that he had to do, that was part of his ordered existence.

Young as he was, there were set ways in which

Evan behaved that were not typical of carefree youth, odd habits and rules to obey, which made him comfortable; to disregard these practices or to flout them would be unlucky, at the least.

One of these rules concerned his shoes. Taken off, at night, say, they must be placed precisely beside one another, left against right, toecaps exactly parallel. The same applied to any sort of footwear, from bedroom slippers to Wellington boots, though these two types were spared the next routine, which applied to the tying of laces. The left shoe must be laced up (and tied in a double knot) before the right, always. The same priority applied with socks – always the left first.

As though to compensate for this preferential treatment, Evan habitually carried his handkerchief in his right trouser pocket, any money in his right jacket pocket, and wore his watch on his right wrist. There were other foibles too, such as tooth-cleaning: for half this exercise, the brush must be held in one hand, for half in the other. Added to all this, Evan was a firm believer in the standard superstitions. He touched wood to avert bad luck of course, he never walked under ladders, he always both bowed and said, 'Good morning, my lord,' on seeing a magpie, and on the rare occasions when he met a chimney-sweep, he did not allow himself to make a wish until he had then seen a dog's tail.

To break any of these, his rules, would have worried him in some degree.

To fail to visit the Roundhill was unthinkable.

It need not be done at the very beginning of the holidays. In fact he liked to postpone the visit as long as he could bear to, to make a treat of it, to be able to think, 'It's still to come.'

So that it was not until the end of the first week of that sunny August of 1936 that Evan allowed himself to make his pilgrimage. Getting out of bed that morning and going to the window and looking across, he told himself that this was the day, that the Roundhill was waiting for him, waiting for his climbing feet.

So he dressed, putting upon those feet the left sock and then the right, slipping his feet into the shoes and lacing and double-knotting them in the same order. He made sure that his handkerchief, some coins and his wristwatch were all in the correct places, and then brushed his teeth in the prescribed manner.

After breakfast, at which, as always, he cut his toast into six exactly equal pieces, he got out his bike and set off. Slung round him was a leather case containing a pair of binoculars that his parents had given him for his twelfth birthday, nearly two and a half years before. Perhaps the greatest pleasure of these visits to the Roundhill was to sit on its summit and be able, looking through these field-glasses, to see his own house. Not only did the magnification allow him to see the building clearly, but even, tiny in the distance, his own bedroom window and the may tree beneath it.

Now he cycled happily through the deserted lanes towards his objective. Quite a number of better-off people now owned motor-cars, but it was still a rarity to meet one in the lanes, and the only noises that Evan heard were those of birdsong, the lowing of cows, and the puffing of a distant train.

Except when momentarily obscured by a high hedge or a clump of trees, the Roundhill was in sight the whole way, and really, Evan thought, I couldn't be much happier than I am this morning.

I know there are things for people to worry about. They think the King wants to marry some divorced American woman. Then there's a lot of talk about this chap Adolf Hitler in Germany, even that there's the chance of another war. But Dad says the last one was the war to end all wars and he was in the Navy so he should know.

'Anyway, there's no point in worrying about any of that,' he said out loud, 'on a lovely morning when there's weeks of the holidays still to go, and I'm riding my new bike that they gave me for Christmas, a Raleigh tourer with three-speed Sturmey Archer gears, on my way to you.' As he looked up towards the Roundhill ahead, a magpie flew across his line of sight and he bowed low over the handlebars and murmured, 'Good morning, my lord.'

Soon he turned off the lane on to a rough track that skirted round the foot of the hill and led eventually to a farmhouse and buildings. Half-way along this track were the ruins of an old field-shed, bramble-covered and almost roofless now. As usual, Evan left his bike within its crumbling walls, and set off uphill towards the topknot of trees above.

He did not expect to meet anyone, in fact he had never met anyone on the Roundhill. Obviously the farmer must tend the sheep that grazed its grassy slopes, but Evan had never come across him. No one else, he liked to think, came here. It was his place.

So it was a surprise for him to catch a sudden glimpse, he thought, of some movement in the fringe of trees. He unslung his binoculars and focused on the spot, but could see no one. Maybe it was the farmer, he thought, or perhaps just a sheep.

Reaching the top, he made straight for his usual viewing-place at the edge of the trees. From here he could look back, due west, at his house. A big beech tree had fallen in a storm some years before, and a section of its trunk, covered in moss and lichen and ivy, made a useful seat.

Sitting down at one end of it now, Evan took out his binoculars again and aimed them westwards. Busy with focusing them exactly and then concentrating on picking out the details of his home and its grounds, he heard nothing.

But then, quite suddenly, he felt a presence.

Lowering the binoculars, he glanced quickly to his left, and there, sitting at the other end of the fallen beech trunk, was a girl. She sat quite still, not looking at him but simply staring westwards as had he.

Evan's immediate feelings were of annoyance, anger even. What did she think she was doing, sitting there on his seat on his hill? Then he thought, perhaps it's her hill or rather her father's, and, feeling that he could not stay silent, whoever she was, he said, 'Hullo. I say, are you the farmer's daughter?'

The girl turned her head to look directly at him. Evan judged that she was perhaps a couple of years younger than himself.

'No,' she said.

'Oh,' said Evan.

He began to feel annoyed again at this intruder. Then what are you doing here, he thought?

'What are you doing here?' he said brusquely.

Her eyes were blue, he thought, and she had long fair hair that hung down her back and was held across the crown of her head by a thin red bandeau.

'I imagine,' she said, 'that I am doing exactly the same as you. I am sitting on top of the Roundhill.'

She knows what it's called, thought Evan.

'Are you local?' he asked.

'I once lived not far away,' she replied, turning her head to look once more to the west.

This gave Evan a moment to study her. Though she was sitting down, he judged her to be tall for her age, perhaps almost as tall as himself. But what puzzled him were the clothes she wore. They seemed strangely old-fashioned. He had seen pictures somewhere of girls wearing clothes like that.

She wore a white dress with short puffed sleeves, caught at the waist with a white sash. Around her collar and again around the hem of her skirt was a pattern of what looked like tiny pink dog-roses. On her legs were black woollen stockings, and on her feet black patent-leather shoes, each with a strap that buttoned over the ankle.

Evan had never before seen a girl of about twelve years old dressed thus, except . . . except in a book that I've got, he thought . . . what book is it? . . . Yes, of course, it's in my copy of *Alice in Wonderland*. That particular edition, given to Evan years before, was illustrated with coloured plates, many of which included pictures of the girl whose adventures Lewis Carroll had chronicled, a girl dressed exactly as was this one!

As she said nothing further, Evan cast about for something to say. We cannot just sit here in silence, he thought, and she doesn't seem in any hurry to go.

Awkwardly now, for he felt he hadn't been exactly friendly, he said, 'Do you come here often?'

'Yes. I do,' she said.

'By the way, my name's Evan,' he said. 'What's yours?'

The girl turned her head again to look directly at him. Her eyes were very blue, he saw now. She smiled.

'My name,' she said, 'is Alice.'

CHAPTER 3

How strange, Evan thought, how really weird.
Those clothes, the eyes, the hair – just like the
pictures in my book. And now the name.
Suddenly, unaccountably, he felt a sneeze
coming on. Shutting his eyes as one does, he
sneezed twice in quick succession, expecting to
hear the girl say, 'Bless you!' as they always did

in his family. But when he looked across at the other end of the beech trunk, there was no one there.

Evan jumped to his feet. Gosh, she must have moved like lightning, he thought, and he hurried into the trees, calling, 'Alice? Where are you? Don't go.' But there was no sign of her.

She must have run right through, he thought. She'll be going down the other side of the hill, and he too ran. But when he emerged from the eastern fringe of the trees, there was nothing to be seen but a few sheep that looked up at him in mild-eyed surprise.

Of course, said Evan to himself, she's hiding behind a tree somewhere. Hide and Seek! Just the sort of game the real Alice would have played. Though what do I mean by the real Alice?

Methodically he hunted among the various trees – beech, ash, sycamore, the odd oak – expecting to come upon the girl at any moment. But the only thing he saw was a squirrel.

Cycling home, Evan puzzled over it all. How suddenly she had appeared, how suddenly vanished. And those clothes, the look of her generally, how odd it all was.

She'd said she once lived near. Where did she live now? She said she came often to the Roundhill. Which means, he thought, that if I go up there again this holidays, she'll very likely be there too. Half an hour ago, this thought would have annoyed him greatly. Now, somehow, he wasn't quite sure.

Curiosity is a strong instinct, with people as with cats, and Evan said to himself that he might like to meet Alice once more. Not that I really give a hoot whether I ever see the girl again, he quickly added, but I would like to find out more about her.

At his bedroom window, the following morning, he trained his binoculars on the Roundhill. At that range it was not possible to distinguish the fallen trunk from its background of trees, but there was a small gap where the beech had originally stood, so he knew whereabouts to look. Had there been a human figure there, he would probably have been able to see it.

There wasn't, of course. What had he

expected? That the girl would already be there? Next thing, he said to himself, you'll be imagining that she's always there, that she lives there.

'Piffle!' he said as he began to get dressed, picking up various bits of clothing from wherever he'd flung them before going to bed. Precise Evan might appear to be, with all his palaver about shoes and tooth-cleaning and toast-cutting, but, those apart, he was a normal untidy fourteen-year-old. The idea of folding or hanging up clothes or of putting them away neatly never occurred to him, and if there hadn't been servants to make his bed each day, it would probably never have been made.

In the middle of dressing, he stopped, one leg in his grey flannel trousers, one out, as a thought struck him. Why had Alice been looking exclusively due west, as he had, looking towards his village? Had she once lived in some other house in it? If so, why had he never met her before? It wasn't a big village; they would have been bound to bump into one another. Perhaps she lived miles away. She couldn't, though, not if she came often to the Roundhill. It's a mystery, he thought as he pulled on his trousers.

'Only one thing to do,' he said as he put on his left shoe, 'and that's ask her.'

'I'm going into town to do some shopping this morning,' said his mother at breakfast. 'D'you want to come, Evan?'

'No thanks, Mum.'

'What are you going to do with yourself then?'

'Go for a bike ride.'

Never before had Evan been to the Roundhill two days running. Never before had he climbed its slopes with such a feeling of excitement. What's the matter with you, he asked himself? Don't tell me you're getting soppy about this Alice girl. She's only a kid.

Reaching the fallen trunk, he did not get out his binoculars as usual but sat sideways on it, his eyes fixed upon the other end where yesterday she had suddenly appeared.

He had timed his arrival to coincide with that of the previous day. Though of course she could come at any time, he thought. With this in mind, he had, before leaving, persuaded the cook to make him some sandwiches. These, together with two bananas and a bottle of lemonade, he had packed in his saddle-bag.

So that now he was prepared to wait, if wait he must, till the girl turned up. In fact he was quite looking forward to having a picnic lunch – though I suppose I'll have to offer to share it, he thought, when she does come.

But 'when' gradually became 'if', as the morning drew on with no company for Evan but sheep.

At first he had remained sitting on the trunk, watching it, but then he began to turn his vigil into a kind of game, a kind of Grandmother's Steps where he would look away for a moment and then suddenly look back, to catch her in the act of her arrival. But she did not arrive. Soon Evan's seat became uncomfortable, and he stood up and began to move about, even going so far as to hunt about once more among the trees, and look down the eastern slopes of the hill. Which is the way she must have come and gone yesterday, he thought.

By eleven o'clock Evan had become hungry. He ate all the sandwiches and the two bananas and drank the lemonade, and sat down again on the trunk. It's no good watching for her, he said to himself. The only way to make her come is to shut my eyes and count to a certain number before I open them again. He counted, first to twenty, then to fifty, then to a hundred, but no one appeared.

Then suddenly Evan thought, felt somehow almost sure, that Alice was there all the time, hidden, watching him. Why? Because she was waiting for him to go, because she wanted the place to herself. He'd come because he wanted to see her again, but she didn't want to see him.

'Stupid girl!' said Evan crossly. 'I'm not hanging about here any longer.'

He picked up the empty lemonade bottle and shoved the paper in which the sandwiches had been wrapped into his pocket. He was about to fling the banana skins away, when he decided to leave a message, just in case Alice should turn up later. Not that he cared, one way or the other, but if she did come, well, she'd know he'd been there.

So he carefully stripped the banana skins into their segments, and laid them upon the beech trunk to form a word.

the banana skins said.

CHAPTER 4

That night Evan had a dream about the girl Alice. He dreamt that he was coming through the lychgate into the churchyard and, looking across, he saw a figure dressed in white sitting on the edge of a big raised stone coffer, black-stockinged legs dangling.

As happens in dreams, he was immediately

standing beside her without the effort of walking there. He saw that she was staring eastwards, and knew of course what she was staring at without the bother of asking her.

'You can see it best from here,' she said. 'Indeed there is a fine view of it between those two great hornbeam trees, is there not?'

He shaded his eyes to look, for the sun had just risen over the top of it.

'Yes,' he replied. 'Somewhere round about here would suit me fine, don't you think?'

She did not answer, and when he turned his head, she had vanished. The top of the stone coffer was bare. He looked at its side, to see who was buried there, but it was so old and the graven lettering so weatherworn that its inscription was illegible. There was lettering on its far side, he found, but that too he could not decipher, except for five words, low down, which he could just make out.

SEEK AND YE SHALL FIND he read.

On waking, the dream was still absolutely clear in his mind, so much so that he had no doubt of finding the stone coffer exactly where he had dreamed it to be.

The Penningtons' house was not far from the churchyard, and after breakfast Evan walked down there. He opened the gates of the roofed wooden lychgate and made his way across, half expecting to see a white-clad figure. But there wasn't one, nor, when he reached that part of the churchyard from which it was possible to see the Roundhill between the two hornbeams, was there a stone coffer, but only a scatter of ordinary gravestones, some upright, some flat.

He walked home again, remembering those five words. One thing's certain, he said to himself. If I don't seek, I won't find, and he fetched his binoculars and got out his bike and set off.

Because she was dressed in those same white clothes, Evan saw her sitting on the trunk long before he reached the summit.

As before, she was looking out westwards, but then she turned and waved at him. Evan waved back, feeling a sudden glow of pleasure, and hurried on upwards, so that by the time he reached the beech trunk, he was a bit breathless.

'Are you all right?' said Alice, smiling.

Strange, thought Evan, it's a nice smile yet somehow it's a sad one.

'Yes,' he said. 'I'm OK.'

'OK?' she said. 'What does that mean? I have never heard that expression before.'

Strange, thought Evan again.

'I'm all right,' he said.

Looking at the far end of the trunk, he saw that the banana skins had gone.

'I was up here yesterday actually,' he said in an offhand manner. 'Matter of fact, I left you a message.'

'I know,' said Alice. 'I saw it.'

'Today?'

'No, yesterday.'

'You were up here yesterday then?'

'Oh yes.'

Evan sat down on the trunk.

'Birds must have taken the skins, I suppose,' he said.

'I expect so,' said Alice. 'Magpies, I dare say.'

'I like magpies,' said Evan. 'They're so bright and bold and cheeky.'

Even as he spoke, one flew across the slopes below them, where the flock of ewes and their lambs of the spring were grazing. It landed on the back of a sheep and stood there, flirting its long tail up and down. A second bird followed, crying its harsh 'chak-a-chak-a-chak'.

'One for sorrow, two for joy,' said Alice.

Shall I do my usual thing, thought Evan? She'll think I'm loopy, but it's bad luck if I don't, so he bowed and called, 'Good morning, my lord.'

'Don't forget the other one,' said Alice. 'It is probably his mate.'

'You're right,' said Evan, and he bowed again and said, 'Good morning, my lady.'

'That is better,' said Alice.

They sat in silence a moment, watching the brilliant black and white birds, and then the girl said, 'Evan?'

Evan's pale face reddened a little at being thus, for the first time, addressed.

'Yes?' he said.

'May I ask a favour of you?' said Alice.

'Yes, do.'

'Might I borrow those spyglasses of yours for a moment? I have never made use of such things.'

'Of course,' said Evan.

He took them from their case and handed them across.

'They're sort of hinged,' he said, 'so that you can fit them against your eyes, and then you move this little wheel thing in the middle to get the focus right. Oh, and you put this leather strap round your neck so's you won't drop them.'

'I shall not drop them,' said Alice.

She stood up and took the binoculars from him, slipping the strap over her head. She walked forward a couple of paces and raised them to her eyes.

'Actually the focus is probably about right,' said Evan.

'It is,' said Alice.

She held the binoculars steady. To Evan, standing behind her, it seemed she was looking pretty well directly towards his house.

Alice sighed, a deep sigh.

'Can you see OK?' asked Evan.

She lowered the fieldglasses and turned to smile at him again.

'Yes, Evan,' she said. 'I can see OK, thank you.'

'You were looking in the same direction I always do,' Evan said, 'to see our house. It's called The Grange. I live down there, you know.'

He pointed.

'See the church,' he said, 'with those two great big hornbeam trees this side of the churchyard?'

She looked again through the binoculars.

'Well, now look to the right a bit. Ours is the next house along, a tall house, three storeys, can you see it?'

'Yes,' said Alice. 'I can see it.'

'You might just be able to pick out my bedroom window. Top storey, facing this way.'

'With a may tree below it,' she said.

'Yes, that's right. But how on earth do you know it's a may tree?' For a long moment the girl did not answer.

Then she said, 'Oh, I thought I saw a pinkish tinge to it. They are remarkably good, these spyglasses. It is amazing what you can see.'

'You can borrow them if you like,' Evan said.

Then she'll have to come here again, he thought, to return them.

'It is indeed kind of you to make such an offer, Evan,' Alice said, 'but I would not think of depriving you of them, even for a short period of time,' and she held the binoculars out towards him.

How strangely she speaks, thought Evan. Even in the dream she spoke in that funny long-winded way.

'Honestly,' he said, 'I can do without them for a bit. You hang on to them.'

'I would not dream of it,' said Alice.

Evan replaced the binoculars in their case.

'Look,' said Alice. 'We have company.' And Evan saw the magpies fly hastily away as the flock began to bunch at the approach of a man with two collies at his heels.

The farmer, thought Evan. He would have to turn up now.

They saw the man send the dogs around the sheep to hold them while he cast an eye over them. Then he called the dogs to heel again, and, as the flock trotted away downhill, came striding up the slope towards the watching boy and girl.

What's he want? thought Evan. I suppose he'll tell us we're trespassing, but we're not doing any harm. On an impulse he moved a pace in front of Alice, as though to protect her.

'Morning, young man,' said the farmer when he reached them. He looked as farmers are supposed to look: big and beefy and red-faced.

'What are you doing up here?' he said.

'We're not doing any harm,' Evan said.

The farmer looked puzzled.

'We?' he said. 'You got a dog with you then? Because if you have, you put him on a lead till you're well clear of my sheep.'

'No,' Evan said, 'I don't have a dog.'

'Well, what d'you mean, "we", then?'

Evan glanced behind him but there was no one there.

'I don't know,' he said.

CHAPTER 5

At breakfast next morning Charles and Barbara Pennington were reading the letters that the postman had just brought.

'Oh dear!' said Barbara as she read. 'Oh well, I suppose we'll have to.'

'Have to what?' Charles asked.

Evan's mother handed the letter to her husband.

'It's from Beatrice,' she said.

Beatrice was Barbara's elder sister, and, unlike her, had a large brood of children, six in all.

'She has to go into hospital,' Barbara said.

Evan's father read the letter carefully, as lawyers are supposed to do.

'Hm,' he said. 'She seems to be in a bit of a hurry about it all. Well, he'll be company for Evan at any rate.'

'Who will?' asked Evan.

Not one of Auntie Beatrice's kids, I hope, he thought. I don't like any of them, specially that Horace.

'Your cousin Horace,' his mother said. 'Auntie Beatrice has to go into hospital for a minor operation and obviously Uncle Rupert can't cope with the children so she's farming them all out. She's asked us to have Horace.'

'For the day?' asked Evan.

'For a week.'

'A week!' cried Evan.

Oh no, he thought, I shan't see Alice for a whole week.

'Yes,' said his mother. 'Like Daddy says, it'll be nice for you, won't it? Horace is just about your age and you can play lots of games together, like tennis and croquet.'

'Horace is no good at games,' said Evan sulkily. 'And I shan't be able to go out on my bike if he's here.'

'Well, hard cheese, old chap,' said his father. 'You'll still have plenty of time for cycling after he's gone back home. There's a lot of your holidays left yet. When are we to have the boy, Barbara?'

'Today, I should think,' said Evan's mother. 'I could fetch him in my car, I suppose, but it would be rather a tiring journey for me. I'll ring up and ask Rupert to drive Horace over.'

I'll go up to the Roundhill this morning, thought Evan, so that I can let Alice know that I shan't be able to come again for a week. But luck was not with him.

After breakfast he hurried to fetch his bike, only to find that it had a flat tyre. Hastily he tried to pump it up, but to no avail. There was, he found, a nail in it. By the time Evan had mended the puncture, he knew that it was too late to go out.

Gloomily he went up to his room and stared out at the distant Roundhill, and then trained his binoculars on its summit. Was that a little flash of white?

Uncle Rupert arrived later that day. He did not stay long, seemingly anxious to be rid of Horace as quickly as possible, and the two cousins were soon left alone together.

They were very unalike, one tall and thin and dark-haired, the other short and tubby with ginger curls and thick horn-rimmed spectacles.

'I say, Evan!' said Horace. 'This is fun, isn't it?'

'Is it?' said Evan.

'I mean, it's jolly nice for me to have a chap of my own age to chat with, my brothers and sisters are all younger than me, you know, it'll be quite a relief to have a week's break from them, and another thing, you and I have never spent much time together, I don't know why, and I'm sure we have lots in common, aren't you?'

'Perhaps,' Evan said.

'I bet there are lots of games we could play,' said Horace. 'Do you play chess?'

'No,' said Evan. 'We could play tennis, I suppose. We've got a tennis court.'

'Quite honestly, old man,' said Horace, 'I'm not much use at games like that, or cricket, or footer. I prefer something less energetic.'

'How about croquet?' said Evan.

'I say, that's a good idea,' said Horace.

They played, and Evan took a most unkind pleasure in roqueting Horace's croquet ball – that is to say, knocking it away all over the lawn and even, if possible, into the shrubberies – and in hearing his cousin's cries of, 'I say, old man! Steady on!'

At lunchtime Horace showed himself in his true colours. He ate two huge helpings of everything, chattering away whenever his mouth was empty enough to allow of speech.

'I say, Auntie Barbara!' he said at the end of the meal. 'That was absolutely scrummy! You're lucky, you are, Evan old man, we don't get grub like this at home.'

By the end of the first day of his cousin's stay, Evan felt exhausted. It would spoil anyone's summer holidays, and especially these ones. I wonder what Alice would think of Horace? I suppose she'd be nicer to him than I am. At least I'm safe from him until tomorrow morning. But he wasn't, because as he was drifting off to sleep, there was a knock on his door.

'Come in,' he called, switching on his bedside lamp.

Horace appeared in the doorway, clad in dressing-gown and striped pyjamas. He blinked owlishly in the light.

'I say, old man,' he said, 'you don't have any biscuits or anything, do you? It seems ages since we had supper. I'm famished.'

'No,' said Evan.

'Well, what time's breakfast?'

'Eight,' said Evan. 'Look, just go back to bed and go to sleep, Horace.'

'All right, old man. Jolly nice to think I've got a whole week here with you. Ah well, goodnight then. We'll have some jolly good chats tomorrow.'

Afterwards, Evan never quite knew how he got through that week with his cousin without going mad. Horace never stopped talking, never stopped eating, never stopped trailing round after Evan wherever he went. Only at night was Evan now safe, for he had made sure that Horace had a supply of biscuits in his bedroom to combat his hunger pangs.

On the day that he had first met Alice, Evan had taken down his copy of Lewis Carroll's story as soon as he arrived home. He had looked through all the coloured plates that illustrated that particular edition.

Alice was on the cover, of course, and on the end papers, and on no less than twenty-eight of the forty-three plates. The one that Evan instantly liked best was that of Alice with the Gryphon.

'Come on!' said the Gryphon, and, taking Alice by the hand, it hurried off.

The picture showed Alice running hard, her fair hair streaming out behind her, just as she must have looked, Evan thought, that day when she was rushing away through the trees.

Each night now since Horace's arrival, Evan had got down the book and turned to this particular picture, and said to himself, 'Only six days more' . . . 'only four days more' . . . 'only two days . . .' Now at long last came the day of Horace's departure.

While Horace was packing his suitcase, Evan's parents took him aside.

'Your mother tells me,' said his father, 'that you haven't exactly gone out of your way to make your cousin's stay a pleasant one.'

'I've played croquet with him hundreds of times,' said Evan. 'He won, once.'

And I've kept the greedy toad supplied with biscuits, he thought.

'I don't understand,' said his father, 'why you have not become good friends. He is your first cousin, after all. Blood is thicker than water.'

'What Daddy is saying,' put in his mother, 'is that when you say goodbye to Horace this morning, the least you can do is to leave him with the impression that you've enjoyed having him to stay.'

'Shake his hand warmly,' said his father.

'OK,' Evan said.

I'd sooner wring his fat neck, he thought.

In the event Evan had little need to speak when the time for parting came, for Horace, true to form, did all the talking.

'I say, I've had a simply spiffing time!' he cried when his father arrived to collect him. 'Thank you very much for having me, Uncle Charles and Auntie Barbara. I shall look forward to coming again very soon, I hope, unless of course Evan can come to stay with us once Mummy is better. I like to think we've become really good chums.'

Evan's Uncle Rupert beamed at this.

'Good show!' he said.

Go, go, go, thought Evan. Get in the car and go. I don't feel guilty at not having been nice to you, Horace. You're so thick-skinned you never noticed anyway.

'Say goodbye to your cousin then,' his father said.

With the greatest of pleasure, thought Evan, and I'll even shake his fat hand warmly.

'Goodbye,' he said.

'I say, cheerio, Evan old man!' cried Horace, and he pumped Evan's arm up and down like someone drawing water from a well. 'I say, I shan't half miss you!' he said.

I shan't miss you at all, said Evan to himself as the car disappeared down the drive and his parents went back indoors.

He raised his eyes to that familiar silhouette on the skyline.

'But I have missed you,' he said.

CHAPTER 6

The next day, as Evan parked his bicycle inside the old broken-down field-shed and began to climb the Roundhill, he told himself that he really must find out more about mysterious Alice, with her strange clothes, and her quaint way of speaking, and her general air of being somehow out of date. She didn't even know what 'OK'

means, he thought. It's almost as though she'd been born ages ago.

When he reached the beech trunk, there was no one on it, so he unslung his binoculars and focused them, as usual, on The Grange.

This time he was somehow not surprised when, lowering the glasses, he turned to find Alice sitting at the other end of the trunk. In every degree she looked exactly the same as when he'd last seen her, white dress, black stockings and shoes, red bandeau over the crown of her head.

'Hullo,' she said.

'Look, Alice,' said Evan hurriedly, 'don't go for a minute. I've got questions to ask you, so please don't just suddenly vanish like you have before.'

'Evan,' said Alice. 'I have all the time in the world.'

'Oh good,' said Evan. 'I'm sorry I haven't come up here this last week but a cousin of mine came to stay and I couldn't get away. We seemed to spend the whole time playing croquet.'

'With the proper mallets and balls, I trust?' said Alice.

'Yes, of course. What else could you play croquet with?'

'Mr Dodgson could tell you that.'

'Who?'

'No matter. But was it not pleasant for you to have a playmate?'

'No,' said Evan. 'I'd much rather have been on my own.'

'Have you no brothers or sisters?'

'No, none. Have you?'

'I had two sisters and three brothers.'

'How d'you mean, you *had* them?'

'Two of the boys died in infancy,' said Alice.

'Oh, I'm sorry,' said Evan.

Alice smiled that slightly sad smile.

'A great deal of water has flowed under the bridge since then,' she said.

She talks in riddles, Evan thought.

'Don't think me nosy,' he said, 'but I really don't know anything about you. For instance, my surname is Pennington. What's yours? Alice who?'

'Alice . . . Hargreaves.'

Why did she hesitate? Evan thought. Is she making up a name for some reason?

'And how old are you?' he asked. 'I'm fourteen, by the way.'

Alice laughed.

'Are you good at mental arithmetic?' she said.

'Not too bad.'

'What would you say then if I were to tell you that I was born in . . . what shall we say . . . 1852?'

Evan grinned. He did a rapid calculation.

'I'd say you were eighty-four years old,' he said, 'though I must say you don't look it. No, seriously, how old are you?'

'Let us say twelve,' replied Alice.

'And where do you live?'

'Where do I live?' said Alice. 'That is a difficult question to answer. At first I lived in Oxford, later in Hampshire.'

'But where do you live now?' persisted Evan. 'I mean, it must be somewhere near or else I wouldn't be meeting you here on top of the Roundhill.'

Alice still did not answer Evan's question

directly. Instead she said, 'For me the Roundhill has ever been a favourite place. Of all my haunts, this is where I always return. I think I inherit from my father a love of high places. He would often quote from the psalms, "I will lift up mine eyes unto the hills from whence cometh my help".'

'Is he a clergyman then?' asked Evan.

'He was the Dean of Christ Church, at Oxford,' Alice said.

Why does she use the past tense, Evan wondered? Is he dead then? Better not ask.

'My father's a lawyer,' he said. 'You looked at our house through the binoculars the other day, remember? I should like to show it to you one day. Do you have a bike?'

'What is that?'

'A bike? A bicycle, of course.'

'Ah, yes,' said Alice. 'No, not as things stand at this moment in my life. Later.'

Another riddle, Evan thought.

'You're a strange girl, Alice,' he said. 'Sometimes I haven't the ghost of an idea what you mean.'

Again Alice smiled.

'One day you will, Evan,' she replied.

'I don't understand,' Evan said. 'Talking to you is rather like being in the middle of a dream.' And then, on impulse, he went on, 'I had a dream about you not long ago. We were in the churchyard.'

'Where you will one day lie,' said Alice.

'Yes, though not till I'm really old, I hope. Eighty perhaps, or more, I like to think, though it's hard to imagine what it must be like to be that age. Can you imagine being that old?'

'Oh yes,' said Alice. 'Very easily indeed, as it happened.'

As it happened? thought Evan. She talks as though she knew.

'You sound as though you knew all about life already,' he said.

'Yet in fact I am very young for my age, Evan,' said Alice. 'As you will one day find out.'

Suddenly she pointed over his head.

'Look,' she said.

Evan turned to look, and there, floating

effortlessly on broad unmoving wings over the Roundhill, was a great hawk.

'A buzzard!' Evan said. 'They're beautiful, aren't they?' But there was no reply and of course, when he looked back, no Alice.

CHAPTER 7

Evan's parents were not as obsessive as their son,
in, for instance, the taking off, putting on or lacing
of their shoes. Nonetheless they liked to live life to
a fairly set routine. When, for example, they
played a game of croquet in the summer it was
almost always after tea on Sunday afternoons –
providing the weather was fine, of course.

During term time Charles and Barbara solemnly played against each other, and in the school holidays Evan joined in. Otherwise, leaving aside the week of Horace's visit, he did not play much, for there was no one to play with.

They usually played three matches in all, rather more by Pennington rules than by those of the All-England Croquet Club, and on the following Sunday things ended in predictable fashion. Evan's father won, his mother came second, and he was third.

Charles Pennington played always with the blue ball. His style was very precise and methodical, and he took pleasure in roqueting the others.

Barbara played with the black ball, and would plead for mercy if about to be roqueted.

'Poor little Blackie!' she would say. 'Don't hit me too far away.' (Meaning 'Don't make me walk to the other end of the lawn – it's so tiring.')

Evan played with the red. The ruthless technique of one parent and the spineless attitude of the other always annoyed him, so that he played with a careless abandon and very seldom won.

Now, at the close of the final game, his father and mother went indoors, and Evan, left alone, began to practise.

He fetched the fourth ball, the yellow, and, lining them all up, played them in turn, aiming either to go through a particular hoop or to hit one of the two pegs. He had struck three of the balls and was addressing the fourth (his own red), when suddenly the yellow ball came speeding back across the croquet lawn and knocked the red flying.

Evan looked up to see Alice walking towards him, mallet in hand.

'Let us have a game,' she said.

'How on earth did you get here?' Evan said.

'Never you mind,' said Alice. 'Come on, I challenge you. I will play with the yellow, I always did.'

Just then Barbara Pennington came out through the French windows and called, 'Evan, do you want a glass of lemonade?'

She seemed to be totally unaware of the girl standing beside him. Evan turned round, expecting that Alice would somehow have done her vanishing trick, but no, there she was, in full view of his mother.

'Yes, please,' Evan said. 'Two glasses, please.'

'Why two?'

'One for me, and,' he pointed at Alice, 'one for her.'

'Look,' his mother said in a bored voice, 'if you want two glasses say so, instead of playing silly games of Let's Pretend. You're too old for that sort of thing. You can fetch your own lemonade.'

'I'm sorry,' Evan said. 'I can't think why my mother was so rude. Why, she acted as though you weren't there.'

'But you know I am,' said Alice. 'So let us play.'

I bet I can beat her, Evan thought. Girls are no good at croquet – she'll be worse than old Horace, I expect.

But in fact Alice won the game quite easily. Her aim was very true, and several times when Evan was in a good position to go through a hoop next shot, the yellow ball would not only knock the red aside but go through itself.

Evan was tempted, though only for a second, to say what his father said on the rare occasions when he was beaten – 'The best man lost' – but as it was he just said, 'You're good,' in a rather rueful voice.

'I've played a great deal with my sisters,' said Alice.

'What are their names?'

'Lorina – she is older than I am, and Edith who is younger. The croquet lawn at our Oxford house was a good one, though this one is perhaps even better.'

She leaned on her mallet and looked around.

'It is a dear old house,' she said. 'I am so glad that it is you who lives in it now.'

'You talk almost as though you had been here before,' said Evan.

'Now how could that possibly be?' said Alice. 'Come, let us have another game. You must get your revenge.'

But once again Evan was soundly beaten.

'I must go now,' Alice said as they laid down their mallets.

'But won't you come in and have some lemonade?' Evan said. 'I'm sure my mother and father would like to see you.'

'If they could,' said Alice, 'I dare say they would but it cannot be done. But you will see me again, will you not?'

'Oh, I hope so,' said Evan. 'I don't go back to school for another eight days. I suppose you'll soon be going back too?'

'Going back,' said Alice, 'is something that I am very used to.'

'I wish we didn't have to,' said Evan. 'Oh dear, how time flies.'

'In both directions,' said Alice.

'What d'you mean?'

'See the may tree,' said Alice, pointing, 'under your bedroom window?'

'Yes,' said Evan, 'but how did you know . . .?'

'You lent me your spyglasses, remember?'

'Oh yes. Well, what about it?'

'Does a thrush still sing in it in the early mornings?'

'Yes, but how . . .?'

'It has grown into a fine tree,' said Alice. 'As you will grow into a fine man, I do not doubt. And now I must leave you.'

Evan swallowed.

'Alice,' he said rather breathlessly, 'I hope we shall keep in touch. I mean, I still don't know where you live, but I hope I shall see you next holidays.'

'Perhaps you will always see me, Evan,' Alice replied, 'in your mind's eye.'

Evan sighed.

'Why do you always talk in riddles?' he said.

Alice smiled.

'Goodbye,' she said, 'for the present.'

'Which way are you going?' Evan asked.

For answer, she pointed towards the Roundhill.

'You're surely not going up there now?' he said. 'It's a good five miles' walk and it'll be dark in a couple of hours. Why not stay the night here? We could put you up.'

'Thank you, no,' said Alice.

'Oh, all right,' Evan said. 'We'll go down through the walled garden. There's a door in the wall at the bottom corner. It's the quickest way into the lane.'

'Yes, I know,' said Alice.

Just short of the door, Evan stopped and said, 'Oh, blow! I've just remembered. Dad always keeps it padlocked. I'll go and get the key.'

He ran off, and then stopped and turned round.

'Shan't be half a tick,' he called.

But Alice was gone.

She's gone through it, thought Evan. Funny, it must have been unlocked all the time.

But when he went back to the gate to open it and call goodbye, he found that it was indeed firmly padlocked.

CHAPTER 8

Much later, looking back to that moment by the garden door, remembering how he had thought, 'She's gone through it,' Evan supposed that it must have been then that he admitted to himself the truth about the girl called Alice Hargreaves.

He walked back up the walled garden and on to the croquet lawn, collecting up the mallets and the four balls. The red and the yellow, he noticed, were side by side as exactly as a pair of his shoes, almost touching one another but not quite.

He ate his supper without tasting it, looked at a book without reading it, and went up to his bedroom. It was still just light enough, before he drew the curtains, to see the Roundhill. He lay in bed, his mind in a whirl.

He thought of Alice who constantly vanished, Alice who talked in riddles, Alice whom his mother could not see. How could she be flesh and blood and yet invisible?

But if she is not flesh and blood, he told himself, then there is only one thing that she can be. And I don't believe in them. Do I?

He remembered her exact words, spoken on the Roundhill. 'Of all my haunts, this is where I always return.' Why? She'd said she lived in Oxford and then in Hampshire. Not here, between the Cotswolds and the Mendip Hills, between the southern edge of Gloucestershire and the northern limit of Somerset.

She half spoke as though she'd once lived in his

house, in The Grange. How could she have? He'd lived there all his life. When at last sleep did come to Evan that night, it was a fitful one, and he woke very early, at first light.

The sun was not yet up, but the Roundhill stood out black against the lightening eastern sky.

I'll go there now, Evan said to himself. I can be there and back before breakfast, easy. She might be there, you never know. If what I'm thinking is right, she doesn't need sleep. But when he neared the top, there was no sign of anyone. Evan stood there a while, looking down westwards at the by now sunlit scene below: the sweep of the land, the river that ran between the two counties, his village, the church and churchyard, The Grange tiny now without the aid of the binoculars he'd forgotten to bring.

He thought of calling out, 'Alice! Where are you? Are you here somewhere?' But then he thought, that's stupid, if she's here, she'll show herself.

He turned to look at the old beech trunk, still half expecting her to appear, and as he did so, he remembered his banana skin message. Could she perhaps have left one for him?

There was nothing on the trunk that he could see, but then he noticed, just in front of it, some pieces of stick, arranged, it seemed in a pattern, though this one

made no sense.

But then, sitting down on the trunk, he saw that he'd been looking at the pattern upside down. Now it looked like this

AL

She has left a sort of message, he thought! But why AL? It should have been AH, for Alice Hargreaves. No, wait a minute, they aren't her initials, they're just the first two letters of her first name, though why she stopped in the middle I don't know.

'I don't know,' he thought as he cycled home, those are the words I'm always saying about her. Shall I ever know?

For the rest of that week, the last full week of his summer holidays, Evan cycled to the Roundhill every day. Every day, though he sat and waited patiently, he had the place to himself. Yet he clearly remembered Alice saying, after their games of croquet, 'But you will see me again, will you not?' And that, Evan said as the week ended, I still believe, whatever she is.

On the next Sunday morning he did not go, because his parents, for unknown reasons, decided to attend church and required him to go with them: nor did he go that afternoon, because he felt that Alice might perhaps appear on the croquet lawn, as she had on the previous Sunday. Which she did not.

Term began on the Tuesday, so now there was only one day of the holidays left. She must come today, Evan said to himself on the Monday morning, and he rode off straight after breakfast, determined to wait out the day if need be.

Parking his bike in the usual place, he began to climb up the grassy slopes, sheep scattering before him. Soon to his joy he saw the familiar white-clad figure sitting and waiting for him. This time she did not wave in greeting but only smiled at his arrival and patted the trunk beside her.

'Sit by me, Evan,' she said, 'for I have one last thing to tell you.'

'What d'you mean?' Evan said. 'We shall meet again, shan't we? Next holidays?'

Alice did not answer this. Instead she said, 'Once upon a time, a long time ago, I stayed at the house of a school friend during the summer holidays. From the window of the bedroom that I was given in that house, there was a wonderful view. It was a view of a very special place where I thought I should like always to be. Wherever I spend my life, I said to myself, and however long that life is, I am determined to come back to that place, even after death. And so it has fallen out.'

Evan opened his mouth to speak, but Alice checked him gently with a raised hand.

'Now at long last,' she said, 'I have met someone to whom that special place, that wonder land, is as precious as it was to me, and so now at last my spirit is at rest.'

'Please,' Evan said, '*please*, Alice, tell me what you mean, what you are. I must know.'

'A book will tell you,' Alice said. 'A biography, that I am sure you will find in your school library. A biography of a certain Mr Dodgson. And of course I am in a book, I have been in that book for seventy-one years. Who knows, I may be in that book for all time. Millions have known me, know me now, will know me in the future. But of all the millions, only you have met me upon a certain round hill.'

'But shall I meet you again?' said Evan.

For answer, Alice pointed down the slopes, and there, flying across them, was a solitary magpie.

For once Evan could not be bothered with the ritual of bowing and declaiming, but of course when he turned to face Alice on the beech trunk beside him, she was no longer there.

Evan watched the magpie hopping about among the sheep. He sighed, a deep sigh.

'One for sorrow,' he said.

Then a second magpie came, and a voice somewhere, a young girl's voice, said, 'Two for joy.'

CHAPTER 9

Early on the following morning the thrush began to sing in the may tree under Evan's window. He woke to the repeated phrases of its familiar song, 'Did he do it, did he do it? Judy did,' and for an instant he felt suddenly as miserable as when he had been only eight and going away to boarding school for the very first time. Because today he must leave not only The Grange and the Roundhill but Alice too. The house and the hill he would see again, the girl perhaps never.

His mood was only momentary. Alice wouldn't want me to feel sad, he told himself, and he concentrated on the thought of going, later that very day, into the school library and, hopefully, finding this biography she'd talked about, of some old chap called Dodgson. Whoever he was, it sounded as though this book might hold the key to everything.

Charles Pennington, leaving, after breakfast, to drive to his chambers, bade farewell to his son in his normal manner. Which is to say that he shook Evan's hand firmly, clapped him upon the shoulder, and said, as always, 'Have a good term, old fellow. Work hard, play hard, that's the ticket.'

Later, Evan said goodbye to the servants. The fat old cook, who had known him all his life, kissed him, the two housemaids looked as if they'd like to, and Whittle the gardener said what he always said, which was, 'Enjoy yerself, Master Evan, and mind and eat up yer greens.'

After lunch, he set off with his mother in her little car, along the road that ran beside the river, giving him a last view of the Roundhill.

Back at school, his mother pecked him on the cheek somewhat absently and said, as usual, 'Goodbye, darling, and don't forget to wear your winter underclothes.'

As soon as he could, Evan went to the library. It was a huge old vaulted building, stocked with many thousands of books, and presided over by the school librarian, Mr Brown.

Mr Brown, who had held this post for as long as anyone could remember, was a short stout old man, remarkable for a large round pink head that was completely bare, like a billiard ball. Generations of schoolboys had, of course, called him Hairy B.

Hairy B. was outwardly grumpy, but in fact a kindly man. Evan now approached him and said, 'Please, sir, do you have a biography of someone called Dodgson?'

'Charles Lutwidge Dodgson, d'you mean, boy?' barked Hairy B.

'Perhaps,' said Evan.

'Look, don't try to be clever, boy,' said Hairy B. 'Dodgson wrote under the name of Lewis Carroll. If you want a biography of Lewis Carroll, say so. It's over there, fourth bookcase along, third shelf, under C.'

Once Evan was sitting down at a reading-table with the biography before him, he turned eagerly to a chapter headed 'The Alice Books'. Now, he thought, this will prove things beyond doubt. If Lewis Carroll's Alice was called Hargreaves, then my Alice is the real one.

But she was not, the book said at that point. She was called Alice Liddell.

Evan felt an enormous sense of disappointment. This girl that he had seen, this apparition, this spirit, was not then the model for the heroine of *Alice in Wonderland*.

But then he began, using the index, to search through the book in quest of the other facts, if facts they were, that Alice had told him in conversation. He remembered them all, clearly.

She had said – as a silly joke of course, he had

thought – that she'd been born in 1852. Alice Liddell had.

She'd said she was the daughter of the Dean of Christ Church, Oxford. Henry George Liddell, Evan read, became Dean in 1855.

Soon he found that Alice Liddell had indeed had two sisters called Lorina and Edith, as his Alice had said.

He recalled her saying, 'I have been in that book for seventy-one years.' He looked up the date of publication of *Alice in Wonderland*. 1865! Exactly right!

Everything was right except for the surname. Why had she called herself that? Would that name be in the index? It was. He turned to the given page.

In the summer of 1880, when she was twenty-eight, Alice Liddell married Reginald Gervis Hargreaves in Westminster Abbey.

Hargreaves was the married name of the woman who had become once more a twelve-year-old girl! She had done so in order to revisit the Roundhill, 'that special place' as she had called it, 'that wonder land'.

His Alice was Lewis Carroll's Alice Liddell, who became Alice Hargreaves!

Lastly he found, in the final chapter of the biography of that Mr Dodgson, whose nom-de-plume was Lewis Carroll, this sentence.

On November 16th, 1934, at age 82, Alice Hargreaves died peacefully.

1934! She had been dead almost two years! Two years towards the end of which her spirit returned to that special place, which, she had told him, she had seen from 'the house of a school friend', with whom she had stayed during the summer holidays.

With hands that trembled a little, Evan turned once more to the index and found, under the letter G, Grange. Turning to the correct page, he read:

In 1864, at the age of twelve, Alice Liddell went to stay with a school friend who lived in the West Country, in a house called The Grange on the Gloucestershire/Somerset borders. In old age, Alice Hargreaves confided that a particular view, from the window of the bedroom in which she had been sleeping during that visit, had been her favourite view in all the world.

'How I wish I could go back there,' she had said, when very near to death.

Evan closed the book. Oh God, he thought, I may not yet believe in you, but thank you, thank you, because you must have had something to do with this miracle. Seventy-two years ago, my Alice stayed in my room in my house. Oh God!

Hairy B. came past, his bald head gleaming under the library lights.

'Found what you want, boy?' he said.

'Yes, thank you, sir,' said Evan. 'I have.'

CHAPTER 10

Sixty-four years later, Professor Evan Pennington sat on a bench in the walled garden of his house, The Grange, enjoying the sunshine.

Over the gate in the wall, he could just see the topknot of trees, much thinner now, on the summit of the Roundhill. A great deal of water had flowed under the bridge since those days when he had been a tall dark-haired boy of fourteen. Now, at seventy-eight, he was rather less tall, for age had shrunk him a little, and his straight hair was snow-white, a lock of it still falling across his forehead.

In between the two ages he had first fought in a World War and then pursued an academic career of some distinction in the field of parapsychology, the study of such phenomena as telepathy and clairvoyance.

In some respects the old man had changed little from the boy. He still placed his shoes neatly together, lacing the left one first, still paid his respects to magpies, and still had not come to terms with that God in whom he wished he could believe as the probable time of his transfer to that reserved site in the churchyard drew nearer.

His parents of course were long dead, as were the fat cook and the two housemaids and Whittle the gardener.

His marriage, in the fifties, had produced one son, and that son in turn married and became the father of a baby girl in 1988. Though Evan played no part in the choice of a name for his granddaughter, he was in no way surprised to be told that she was to be called Alice.

Now, in the summer of the year 2000, the Professor idly scuffed the gravel of the path before his bench, marking out with one heel the letters A.L.

His granddaughter, now aged twelve, was staying at The Grange, and, hearing her calling, he shouted, 'I'm here!'

Alice Pennington came running down from the croquet lawn. Dark-haired, as her father was and as her grandfather had once been, and brown-eyed, she bore no physical resemblance to that other Alice of long ago, that Alice whom Evan had never again seen but had never forgotten. And how different her clothes were – a T-shirt emblazoned with the name of the latest pop group, old jeans, and trainers.

'A.L.,' said the girl when she reached Evan. 'What are you writing, Gramps? Are you spelling my name?'

Evan smiled, remembering the pattern of sticks in front of the beech trunk, all those years ago.

'Actually,' he said, 'they are someone's initials.'

'Whose?'

Evan rose to his feet and took his grand-daughter's hand, and as they walked out of the -walled garden together, he said, 'It's a strange story, darling, and one you may find it difficult to believe. As indeed I myself still sometimes do. But I'll tell it to you if you like, this afternoon, at a special place.'

'Where, Gramps?' Alice asked.

Her grandfather pointed towards the Roundhill.

'Up there,' he said.

After lunch they drove through the lanes, traffic-ridden now, and then turned along the farm track, where Evan parked his car beside the collapsed rubble of what had once been the field-shed. Now, he needed a walking-stick for the climb, and was glad at last to reach the spot where the old beech trunk had lain. It had long rotted away, but the grass was dry, so they sat, facing west, and Evan handed the binoculars to his granddaughter.

'See The Grange?' he said, pointing.

Alice focused on the distant house.

'Yes, and I think I can even see the window of the bedroom I'm in, with the may tree under it.'

'It used to be my room,' Evan said.

Alice lowered the binoculars.

'When you were a boy?' she asked.

'Yes.'

'Is that when it happened? This story you said you'd tell me, about A.L.?'

'Yes,' said Evan. 'I've never told a living soul about it before, but perhaps you are the right person to hear it.'

So they sat side by side on the top of that round hill that had always meant so much to Evan Pennington, and he told his granddaughter every single thing that had happened during those summer holidays in 1936.

When he had finished, Alice sat silent for a time.

Then she said, 'So she was the same age as I am now?'

'Yes.'

'And she actually slept in the bedroom where I am now?'

'Yes. Does that worry you?'

'No, oh no, Gramps,' said Alice. 'And I'll never tell anyone, not even Mum and Dad. It'll just be a secret between you and me.'

She reached out and took hold of her grandfather's hand and gave it a squeeze.

'Oh,' she said, 'how lucky you were to have known her.'